Critical Acclaim

"Mouron is a revelation. He juggles characters with ease in a seamy world perfectly evoked and all of it is done in a tauttempo style"

Huffington Post

"Mouron...writes rough material in a small, confined spaces. His writing is astonishing in his mastery and freshness."

20 Minutes

"...readers will recognize Mouron's portrayals of 'simple folk, disturbed life' who commit only rational murders, justified by drunkenness or necessity and tempered by tears and regrets."

PW

"After Joel Decker, here is the latest literary sensation from Switzerland: brilliant..novelist Quentin Mouron...garnered ecstatic reviews in the French-speaking world.

Goodreads

"There is this "raw" element to this book that made me like it and picture a Tarantino film playing in my head."

Reviewer

"You have to imagine yourself before a scene in a theatre. A scene which would have been built with a few pieces of wood, in a deep snow situated n a remote and lost Quebec village...It leaves a bitter and vivid after-taste, like the morning after a sleepless night."

Le Temps

"(Mouron)...is something else! The writing is terse, the pacing immaculate and the book's atmosphere extraordinary..."

Turnaround

Notre-Dame-de-la-Merci

Notre-Dame-de-la-Merci

By

Quentin Mouron

Translated by Sheila Fischman and Donald Winkler

Library and Archives Canada Cataloguing in Publication

Title: Notre-Dame-de-la-Merci / Quentin Mouron;
        [translated by] Donald Winkler, Sheila Fischman.

Other titles: Notre-Dame-de-la-Merci. English

Names: Mouron, Quentin, 1989- author. | Winkler, Donald,
        translator. | Fischman, Sheila, translator.

Description: Translation of: Notre-Dame-de-la-Merci.

Identifiers: Canadiana (print) 20190196378
            Canadiana (ebook) 20190196432

ISBN 9781771613248 (softcover) ISBN 9781771613262 (PDF)
ISBN 9781771613255 (HTML)

Classification: LCC PS8626.O88 N6813 2020
              DDC C843/.6—dc23

Published by Mosaic Press, Oakville, Ontario, 2021

MOSAIC PRESS, Publishers
Copyright © Mosaic Press 2021

Cover Design by Andrea Tempesta

We acknowledge the support of
Ontario Creates

Funded by the Government of Canada
Financé par le gouvernement du Canada

MOSAIC PRESS
1252 Speers Road, Units 1 & 2
Oakville, Ontario L6L 5N9
phone: (905) 825-2130
info@mosaic-press.com

Books by Quentin Mouron

Au point d'effusion des égouts, La Chaux-de-Fonds, Suisse, Olivier Morattel Éditeur, 2011, 144 p., préfacé par Pierre Yves Lador (ISBN 978-2-9700701-5-3).

Notre-Dame-de-la-Merci, La Chaux-de-Fonds, Suisse, Olivier Morattel Éditeur, 2012, 120 p. (ISBN 978-2-9700701-7-7).

La Combustion humaine, La Chaux-de-Fonds, Suisse, Olivier Morattel Éditeur, 2013, 113 p. (ISBN 978-2-9700825-5-2).

Trois gouttes de sang et un nuage de coke, Paris, France, La Grande Ourse Édition, 2015, 224 p. (ISBN 9791091416368).

L'Âge de l'héroïne, Paris, France, La Grande Ourse Édition, 2016, 134 p. (ISBN 9791091416467).

Trois gouttes de sang et un nuage de coke (Édition poche), Paris, France, Éditions 10/18 [archive], 2015, 224 p. (ISBN 9782264067913).

Notre-Dame-de-la-Merci (Traduction allemande), Zurich, Suisse, Bilgerverlag [archive], 2016, 96 p. (ISBN 978-3-03762-058-8).

Three drops of blood and a cloud of cocaine (Traduction anglaise), Londres, Grande-Bretagne, Bitter Lemon Press, 2017, 260 p. (ISBN 9781908524836).

Drei Tropfen Blut und eine Wolke Kokain (Traduction allemande), Zurich, Suisse, Bilgerverlag, 2017, 240 p. (ISBN 978-3-03762-068-7).

Vesoul, le 7 janvier 2015, Dole, France, Olivier Morattel Éditeur, 2019, 120 p. (ISBN 978-2-9562349-2-0).

Heroïne (Traduction allemande), Zurich, Suisse, Bilgerverlag, 2019, 124 p. (ISBN 978-3-03762-078-6).

Quentin Mouron – A Biographical Sketch

"In 1992, the professional ambitions of his Father, the painter Didier Mouron, took Quentin and his family beyond the Swiss border. They depart to Quebec where they will remain until 2002. And so, Quentin Mouron spends a solitary, peaceful childhood, left to his own devices, in a small rural village some two hours north west of Montreal, with a population of some 900 people, in the heart of Quebec woods. In 1998, Quentin Mouron acquires Canadian nationality.

Returning to Switzerland in 2002 with his family, Quentin Mouron is educated at Oron-la-Ville, before entering high school at La Cité (2004). His first year must be repeated, but ends in a year-long trip to North America (particularly Arizona), where Quentin for the first time encounters the desert, and begins to take its measure: if the forest attracts him, it's in these great arid open spaces that his solitude can find true expression.

After one year, Quentin returns to Switzerland and finishes school (2009), cited for his accomplishments in the French language. But while his classmates turn towards universities in Switzerland and elsewhere, Quentin, not drawn to further studies, repeats his desert experiences – he flies off to California. There he will stay for a year, and will twice cross the American continent. Very early on, Quentin will undergo his literary initiation, and will devour, without always understanding them well, Voltaire, Nietzsche, Sade, Proust, or Oscar Wilde. At the same time, he takes up his pen, and writes his first poems at the age of fourteen.

As he grows older, his literary tastes mature, as does his writing. His book collection grows, with an special place reserved for Albert Cohen and Antonin Artaud, for Dostoyevsky's novels and the thought of Edmund Husserl. Quentin writes short stories, poems, and eventually, during his last pourney, ventures a novel, which he finishes in July of 2011, with the title *Au point d'effusion des* égouts. He then he writes his second novel, *Notre Dame de la Merci*, which is favourably received. (*Le Matin, Le Temps, Le Nouvel Observateur*, etc.)

In March, 2013, Quentin Mouron receives the Alpes-Jura prize for his first novel, awarded in Paris by the jury of the *Associations des* écrivains *de langue française* (*A.D.E.L.F*). He is also invited to Paris, on June 1, 2013, to participate in the *Nuits de la Poésie*. In September his third novel, *La Combustion humaine*, is released: its satirical bite – aimed at the Swiss literary world, but also at the media and social networks – garners him considerable enmity from Swiss writers and journalists, while critics and the general public consider that *La Combustion humaine* is his most impressive work to date.

In 2015, Quentin Mouron publishes *Trois gouttes de sang et un nuage de coke* with the Éditions de la Grande Ourse (Paris). The book is a critical success and is released in soft cover with the Éditions 10/18, as well as being translated into English (Bitter Lemons Press, 2017). In 2016, Quentin Mouron publishes *L'Age de l'héroïne* with the Éditions de la Grande Ourse.

In January, 2019, he publishes *Vesoul, le 7 janvier 2015*, with the Éditions Olivier Morattel (France).

Mosaic Press gratefully acknowledges the support of the
Swiss Arts Council Pro Helvetia Foundation for the translation
of this book by Sheila Fischman and Donald Winkler.

swiss arts council
prohelvetia

Notre-Dame-de-la-Merci

PROLOGUE

"Here...Adam remembers the dust if his natal clay"
From a poem by Mahmoud Darwish,
State of Siege

A November morning. The first flakes are falling onto the Quebec woods . Old man Pottier has known trouble. Trouble that consumes people and things, forests – and that sweeps away snow. Silent, agonized troubles that you can't talk about because the words aren't there, they have never been there. The flakes settle onto the tops of trees, where they want to come to rest – winter is setting in. And in the old man's ashen room, he's in his Sunday clothes. The wind is whistling through an open window and down the chimney. The car is covered in snow. Poets call it a veil or a shroud. Old Pottier is swaying. The cold has wormed its way into his body. Through his Sunday clothes, through the cloth, right to the bone, past all his life's defences. You have to have known a Quebec winter to truly know winter. A three-day storm, and the night when the high tension wires give way under the weight of the snow. You have to have driven the black icy roads. You have to have heard the trees snapping and creaking in the cold. Old Pottier had been a bridge worker. He'd had a wife who drank.

He'd beaten her. They'd had a first son, Jean. And then other children. She'd got ugly. He'd got fat. They'd come to live by the shore of Lac-en-Croix, up north, in the township of Notre-Dame-de-la-Merci. He'd fished. She'd knitted. And then she had died. And he'd wept. The snow falls and blankets everything. At Chertsey a truck hit a pylon. Houses went dark. Old Pottier is swaying, hanging by the neck from an exposed beam. He could have left a note. He'd have liked to. But he didn't know what to write and what was the point. Silence was better. Swirling snow.

Suicides, it's strange how they grip you in your bones and cling and throb deep down. I've known suicides. And they all heap blame on me, insults, barbs that skim the surface, flush with the fog. Often during a storm, you seek those you miss, those you've lost, and you call for them to return, come back, but they're already far away, beyond the snow, too cold, they've vanished. I've known some of those who cried out in the dark, who'd never known what to say but had cried out all the same. If they're dead it's, of course, their own fault.

I don't know if I should go any further at this point in the story. It might be better to stop. Take the time to bury old Pottier, to give voice only to silence. To leave you with your own private tremors. Why not? There are other books. By other writers. Only precise moments in time are not exchangeable.

CHAPTER 1

Odette is sitting in a corner of the dining room, near the cold heater. The power's been off for an hour. She's put a log in the stove and pulled on a coat. Beside her there's a low wooden table and on it, small envelopes filled with cocaine.

Odette's chalet is one of the nicest around Lac-en-Croix. Three floors. Two garages. And a garden she cultivates in the summer. The trees are trimmed. The inside is comfortable, with paintings on the walls. True, it's dark, but Odette needs to be at peace. She wants no prying eyes. No one sticking their nose into her affairs.

She's been in prison, it was a few years ago. She doesn't want to go back. That was enough. How they made fun of her! How they tormented her! It wasn't a very long sentence, she hadn't been found with much. But ten days or ten years. The mere thought of bars...

She runs her hand over the low table, counts the envelopes with her index finger, and tells herself that it's all right, everything's there.

On the wall, facing her armchair, there is a tacky watercolour that she dusts every morning. She bought it when she moved here with her husband. I don't understand what she sees in it. She looks at it every day, for minutes at a time, sometimes an hour. She stares at it

1

particularly when she's upset. The colours are faded. The canvas is stained by the coffee that spattered it when she threw a cup in a rage one day. It should have gone to the cellar long ago. It's a sunset. On a lake. She doesn't know which. Just that she bought it in a junk shop. And when anyone asks her about the painting, she shrugs and says that it's a souvenir from "back then." And if the visitor asks if it was a good time, Odette says no, it wasn't any happier than it is now. And changes the subject. Because she doesn't want to think about it. And also, because she doesn't talk easily about her feelings. If someone persists, probes, pushes her too far, Odette can easily raise her voice, explode, and send them packing.

*

Notre-Dame-de-la-Merci is five hundred inhabitants scattered through the forest down two long gravel roads. Living there are some peaceful retirees. A few families. There are no businesses. No restaurants. There's a church and a school. The local library and a big playground. There is still the village hall they call the "big hall." Together, they make up the town centre.

Odette and her husband came there twenty years ago, to find peace. The city was driving them mad. Always someone brushing up against you. They couldn't stand it. She said that people touched her in the subway, that she was insulted, and every night her husband claimed, coming out onto rue Saint-Denis, that they'd tried to kill him, that he had been lucky to escape. The crowds were too much for them. So, they left for the countryside, the forest, because city dwellers think the country is more peaceful. But in the case of Odette and her husband, they were the ones not at peace. He'd said,

"Odette, I don't feel safe here anymore, I'm suffocating, we've got to leave." So, with the help of one of his buddies, they got a chalet in Notre-Dame-de-la-Merci. A big, beautiful chalet that was the envy of everyone. They weren't rich, but they'd been dealing drugs long enough that they could buy something for themselves.

*

On my road there were two old sourpusses, both loathsome – neighbours. They'd bought a stretch of land in the north to be at peace, but they got into arguments from the very first day. Over what, I don't know. Trifles. So, the first one built a metal fence, very high, to divide the two lots. The second put up barbed wire. One bought a 2000-watt spotlight that he directed at the neighbour's bedroom window. The other bought a 3000-watt spotlight. And things escalated so quickly that midnight came to look like the middle of day. One fired twice at the other's roof one night when he was drunk, and the other, also drunk, fired back. The police came. They spent three months in prison. And when they got out, the fight went on. I remember being asked to sign something, a kind of petition, stating that one of the neighbours was better than the other. And then one got cancer. Afterwards, I don't know, there are different stories... That he was drunk by the side of a road and got hit by a truck, or that he threw himself into its path. Anyway, it was one of the twelve ton's wheels that did him in.

Frankly, there's nothing here that looks like a crime scene. It's a village where you go to retire.

*

Odette and her old man were like every failure, people who know they've missed out on something, that life has kept them at arm's length – and that it will box them forever into a zone of adversity.

They were old Pottier's neighbours. They knew each other. Sometimes they talked. Exchanged the dreary words that neighbours trade with one another. About the weather. When it's likely to change tomorrow, when it changed yesterday. And then each went his own way. Odette's husband got in his car. Old Pottier the same. One went to sell dope. And the other to fish. Old Pottier knitted slippers. Odette stayed home, worried sick. And everything continued on in silence. With no one knowing anything.

Odette's husband was a member of the Hell's Angels. He died in a dumb motorcycle accident. He was leaving a bar, he was drunk. Hit a moose. An antler punctured his belly and he was left there, bleeding, moaning his life away. When Odette heard about it, she felt betrayed. She would have preferred a gunfight. She'd seen gangster films set in New York or Chicago. She envied the women, solemn and gorgeous in their pain, with their big shot men gunned down. But Odette wasn't sad, and she'd never been beautiful. She was ashamed, that's all.

With her husband dead, she kept on dealing. She left the club. The club, anyway, had no more use for her. It was fine when you were "the wife of." But when it was just Odette, she was given to understand that she'd be better off carrying on alone. Which is what she did.

She didn't really love her husband. I mean with a mad and passionate love, but she had a kind of soft spot for him, and he had the same for Odette, a soft spot without any love. "So, we got along. We were on the same page. You know," she said to me, "we weren't hard on each other, so even if people were hard on us, even if they gave us a bad time and we were far from happy, we could at least stick together, have a common cause, and back home, mutually spill our guts." For her love came later. Like salt on a wound.

When her husband was still around, no one in Notre-Dame-de-la-Merci dared to say out loud what they thought. They weren't downright polite, but they choked back their insults in case the guy pulled a gun. Once she was alone all bets were off. They insulted her as much as they liked. "On my way out of Provigo this fat cow comes up and starts badmouthing me, says I'm a scumbag, a poisoner, I'll end up in the electric chair." Maybe the fat woman was crazy. But that someone had dared to accost her like that, drag her through the mud in front of families, to defile her, that is something she can't shrug off.

Odette is not what she dreams of being. She'd like to be taken seriously. To be respected and feared. Sometimes at night she imagines that she's on her way into a room full of tough guys who are putting the fear of God into everyone. They go silent. They shut their mouths when she appears. She intimidates them. Maybe she gives orders to one or the other? Gives a clear sign, agreed on in advance, and the tough guys do as they're told. Always gangster films... But in the morning, when she wakes up, she has to acknowledge where she is. At Notre-Dame-de-la-Merci, in a cottage, with her husband dead, killed by a moose. She, Odette, has served so little time that people look down on her – and what's more, I'll come to this later, she's in love with a good-for-nothing – and this good-for-nothing despises her, steals from her, and hurts her.

*

Notre-Dame-de-la-Merci is an arbitrary choice. Quebec as well. The New World. I invite you to throw back your shutters to see whether across the way, by chance, something is happening. To see if my book, with its dose of cunning and the tricks of art, is a commentary thereon, if my book is something you might come across at your neighbour's who's in tears, your neighbour who drinks. Cities are paved with what's in the news. And the pavements are all nameless and indistinguishable. We walk over them unthinking. Maybe they'd like to be more visible, occupy more space, trip you up so you'd have to take notice? Doubtless they'd love to have you acknowledge them. The city's pavements are crying out to you. They are there with evidence we choose to ignore. And we buy novels that are better written, where nothing smells bad. But there are far more stories than there are readers.

*

Odette makes herself a coffee. Adds a drop of rum. Then sits down again.

They have no children, didn't have the time, or the desire. There were only those of one of his sisters, who stopped by to drop them off without a word, two boys and a girl, and to pick them up two weeks later – still without a word. Motherhood never appealed to her. "It's bad enough just having to drag yourself around," said her man. And with kids, besides, it made no sense. They wouldn't be happy in any case. So, he talked about Fate. "Our dice are loaded, Odette," he said. Adding that there was nothing you could do but wait, like it or not, and to deal with things as they were. And he carried on with his schemes. Because the taste of steak gave his life some meaning, and if they were going to be unhappy, better be unhappy on a full stomach.

He was violent. But Odette didn't get the brunt of it. When he bloodied faces it was outside the house. He was ruthless with anyone who didn't pay. When he got home, he was exhausted. So, he cried. Said that life had, once and for all, left him with nothing good. He didn't rightly know where his pain came from, or the source of his rage or his black heart. He couldn't come up with a reason. He fell back on life in general, on the angels, on Destiny. On crude forays into metaphysics. Said that if he'd been happy, he would never have stooped to extortion, or beaten anyone up. All that, as it were, fell from the sky. Which was convenient for his conscience...

Odette was more practical. Destiny seems to her to be a huge scam. The Good Lord and the angels. Life making excuses for itself. She doesn't believe in it. She blames her sadness on others, on men. The old woman at the cash who humiliated her. The gas jockey who winked at her. Those who laugh when she goes by, who double over with laughter. And then the big guy she loves, who she's ashamed of, and who makes her suffer. The wind's whistling louder. It's cold. The stove can't keep up. She goes looking for blankets in the cellar.

*

You mull things over when it snows, the punishing gusts. Odette has nothing more to hope for. Nor do I have any hopes for her. Hope is a slave to circumstance. The wind has snuffed out everything in her breast. The night rises within her, ice rips at her insides. What does she want? Her shame is like a fog. In the midst of which is a face, ruddy, two dark eyes – a face that glows.

The mad flame of a love spurned, a love that seethes. An impossible love.

*

A cry held back is just more silence. People crowd the streets, the subways, the factories, insubstantial beings who brush against people and walls. Who say nothing. Who constantly hunker down. Some are squeezed into suits, others into blue work clothes, still others have been silent all their lives and wear slippers to muffle their footsteps. Their hair is white. Their bodies dry. Their eyes befogged. And the rope around their necks loose, like the tie you unknot on the way home from work.

This woman on the subway, ugly and insignificant. Dyed hair with streaks, extensions, mascara, a piercing, rouge, blue eye shadow, a facelift, curls, a diamond, a fake Vuitton, mittens, a lovely coat, a skirt, leopard skin tights, trendy boots, and a case for her iPhone. Her old man facing her bored to death. Like her. They say nothing to each other. Haven't for a long time. So drab that I'm surely the only one who remembers them.

*

Still, Odette had, I believe, a romantic childhood, happy, and with dreams. The dreams of a child. In other words, dreams that might come true. For which it's not too late. The future, the real future, belongs to childhood. Then, one day, you wake up an adult – and you know you're an adult because the present makes the future look ugly in your eyes. Wrenches it out of shape. When did things go bad? I don't know exactly. For me I know precisely, but not for Odette. I've tried to imagine her as a child. Chic, merry, less thin and less drugged. With stories of Prince

Charming and dolls, but also, perhaps, dark thoughts. Childhood is very serious. What were her dreams? What became of them? When did her heart shrivel up?

I asked her these questions, indirectly. She replied as well, indirectly. She said she didn't want to talk about it. From the discomfort the memory brought with it, I deduced that there was a wide gulf between those two periods in her life.

*

Odette is in love. A post-widowhood infatuation that has become a tragedy.

She loves Jean, old Pottier's son.

CHAPTER 2

Daniel promised Odette that he would come.

He's the village snow remover. One of those poor bastards who gets up early and goes to bed late, who earns nothing. On the roads every morning from five o'clock, in winter thirty below, thirty-five, the road gliding away under you. You pass house after house, chalets, pushing the snow, a pile here, a pile there. At night you go home exhausted, done in. The snow is heavy. And all the idiots that complain, wanting their pile over here, no, no, farther from the window, don't hide the view, and who gripe at his being late, they should have done it themselves, got it going by hand. And then the crazies. The loonies who expose themselves, the violent ones, the bigots.

Odette doesn't like him, he's a cretin. That's what they say in the village, that he's an idiot. But Daniel is loyal. She knows she can count on him. That he'll be there soon. Which makes her feel good, buoys her up, not a lot – imagine how it feels to be adored by idiots when the ones you love don't give you the time of day. I know what it is to have strangers showering you with flowers when the heart you want to touch stays stubbornly closed. When my first novel came out, my publisher said there you go, you can send out the invitations, and then there I created a Facebook event to which I invited over five hundred people. I had to admit to myself that actually I was inviting only one – and she never replied.

Deep down, Odette feels things. How much he likes her. How she can still have an effect on him, on Daniel, despite her wrinkled face. When she speaks to him he goes red, he stutters, he doesn't know what to say. He'd like to disappear – you can tell when someone wants to disappear. He'd like not to be there in front of her, or rather he'd like it not to be him there with her, but someone else: he's ashamed. Odette knows it. She capitalizes on it. He doesn't see. He's not aware. That means making an ass of himself trying to please her. He'd like her to think of him a little, sometimes, at night – like it if things were not so one-way. When he thinks of Odette, Daniel doesn't just say to himself: there's Odette. He wonders what she's doing, where are you, with whom, who are you thinking of? So sometimes, when it's very dark, Daniel puts himself at the head of in line, the fool. Believes she's thinking about him. That's what comes over him at night. When he can see nothing. When he can imagine anything. When the world assumes the colours that he gives it.

Odette hears a motor.

*

Daniel gets out of his pickup – a rusty old truck with a shovel welded to the front, that belonged to his father. He's wearing a black tuque pulled down over his ears. His beige jacket, full of holes, filthy. Looking like he's got the wrong address. As usual. Short. Somewhat agitated. Stocky. Undecided. Maybe he should retrace his steps? He hesitates, seems to not feel the snow, the wind, engrossed by something within him, weighed down by an idea. Finally, he comes to a decision, makes his move.

He climbs the stairs. Odette senses his emotion. His hesitation at every step. And every step is a new problem, different from the last. Should he keep going or turn around? He wants to see her, it's true, he feels good... But at the same time, he asks himself if she really wants to see him, or if maybe he should come later? But since she called him... Yes, but she didn't say when ... Not exactly... He hesitates. One more step. And if she said no? If she didn't let him in? One more step. He just doesn't know. He should have tidied himself up... Dressed. But he doesn't know how. He's never "dressed himself up to go out." That is, he has gone out, of course, literally, outside his house. But he's never had an opportunity... A burial, once, his father. But he was still very young. Will Odette open her door?

Having reached the door, he's surprised to have climbed so far. He takes a deep breath, the cold enters his body, refreshes him, calms him down. He knocks on the door. She answers.

She's there facing him. Stares at him. He trembles. The problem presents itself once more. He's ill at ease, he doesn't know what to say, struggles for words. Odette lets him in. He crosses the threshold, shivering. An idea comes to him. What he'd like to say. All the feelings locked up inside, that bring tears to his eyes at night. But the words don't come. They turn him down. Leave him in the lurch, just on the brink of expressing himself. All he's left with is the violence of his feelings without the sweetness of poetry, the little words you repeat at night, the "I love yous" that bring peace because they come from within. Everything inside Daniel is thrumming away. She offers him a drink. Tea. He blushes. He accepts.

*

Odette talks business. Reminds Daniel of how he was hired. Of what she promised him. That he would make deliveries. And in exchange she would help him win a court case. Daniel is uneasy. Because of Odette first of all, and then because of the trafficking. He doesn't want to, never wanted to. But he had no choice. He feels trapped. Compromised. Soiled. He'd like to say something too. He starts to talk... stammers... then falls silent. Odette shoots him a glance. It's clear. There's nothing to discuss. It's too late, Daniel, you hear, it's too late... He accepts the drugs.

Then Odette starts to talk to him, almost a monologue. How's his mother doing? The children? The neighbours? She laughs, loudly, roars with laughter. She never talks to Daniel about her unhappiness. Or to anyone else. She pretends. She suppresses the violence. Smooths her mask. While he, he listens. Mainly, he watches her. He tries to reply to her. Sometimes he succeeds. Other times it sticks in his throat – he can't even come up with an idea. And Odette babbles on, about this, about that, she saw one neighbour, then another, a deep thought, a bit of humour, a flash of wit. She censures this one slightly, lays into that one. And she talks too about the weather. As if everything were normal. As if she were not in a state of despair. As if she were feared. Not letting anyone get the better of her. Above all, don't let anyone get the better of you. And this anyone is Jean Pottier. "Winter won't last this year, I'm sure, a few flakes, the same in February, another squall, and that's it. You won't have to push yourself too hard, you'll see, nothing to worry about." And she almost giggles! A big smile.

At the end of the interview, Odette again tells him two or three things about the deliveries, gives him some advice, warns him about the Bérangers, who she knows are capable of anything. And don't stay too long at the fat woman's. And be careful not to get robbed. Don't be taken in by deadbeats. Because there will be some. When her husband was alive, he used his fists, and that was it. He had the whole gang behind him. But when Odette threatens them, they laugh it off. Daniel takes everything in and leaves as if nothing has happened.

*

I keep close to me the one who speaks and tells stories in my place. I know these people. Odette and Daniel are two silent shriekers, two of the defeated. They'd like to howl with all they've got. To make the noise they need to make. To hit the right note, find the perfect pitch that will say who they are, and more: that they exist. I can say, because I've known them, that within themselves they are atremble with life, electric, that they'd love to break free, and that they are rich with colour. Today's painters are wrong when they depict automatons, philosophers. When they draw grey crowds: in the subway, in the factory, at the office. When they deprive them of colour. But, they say, that's the way they are, our eyes are penetrating, perceptive, if they were really alive, we would have caught that but instead, society has murdered them. Have they really come in the back door though? Have they turned them around? Has one of them, or another, gone to the trouble of scratching away the grey surface, as one does with lottery tickets, with a coin, to see what's underneath? Odette and Daniel are silent. They're not dead. They are alive. Behind the silence there are often warring cries. Then they swallow them back. Cave in. Cancel each other out. And the mechanical gestures return, the greyness in the subway, in the factory, at the office. At night, however, the workers are sometimes ready to explode, their limbs tense – and then nothing, they go back to sleep. The rage to live erupts like a belch, it's unsightly – and they choke it back one more time.

I have no mysteries for the reader. Odette loves, Daniel loves. And all of that makes for despairing cries in their breasts that tear them apart and unnerve them, violent cries like the coughs of a tubercular. I myself have loved greatly, far too greatly, and I've written a book, a novel, which I dedicated to a woman who'd devoured me. But Odette and Daniel won't write a book. They will not pose on the set of a TV show. They have only two choices: swallow things back or explode. Because one day, when "the cup runneth over," a stormy day, then the silence will arm and harden itself – and hone its edge. And it will become lethal.

*

Daniel begins his round. He doesn't plough the snow. He pretends. You only plough the snow when it's stopped falling. Before, it's pointless, since it goes on falling and you have to start over. But he still has his orange light, his revolving light. And he moves ahead slowly. And carefully, even if he has a knot in his stomach. If anyone asks him, he will say that he's going to negotiate a contract, to get paid. Something credible. For a long time people haven't been paying him, or have paid him only half, he's always being told how well he's being treated, how shoddy his work is. People say they'll hire someone else who costs less, is more skilful, more organized, more agreeable. You didn't put the snow where you should have! I said on the left! The left! And then, every time, they renew his contract. And they do it, lording over him as if offering him charity, with contempt. Deep down I think they like him fine all the same, that they liked him at least before all that... The elderly were touched by his manners, very correct, his hesitant and respectful air. He was asked to sit down, have a coffee, a slice of cake. Now, of course, things have changed. Silence has descended. They don't even open their doors. They whisper, they spy from inside, to see if he's doing the work, if he's quick enough, and they wait for him to finish. While out in the cold he has only his thermos of tea.

I find him sighing now and then, his eyes misty. He knows perfectly well that he never amounted to much, but now he's even less. There's no more respect in the eyes of the retirees who employ him. They're retired and worthless, certainly, and angry. But they were his people, who encouraged him, who valued him, who bartered their affection. And all that was clear. Daniel enjoyed the compliments of the old ladies, who pushed his way a plate of biscuits, a cup of coffee. The old men who talked to him as to a child, gave him advice, a smile, made a face, pinched his cheek. It was a soft pillow, all the same, where he could rest his head.

*

Daniel starts his deliveries with those at the end of the lake. The Bérangers. Who give him a cold welcome, between two doors that slam – who take the dope and pay the money. The woman threatens from a window to report him to the police, to spill the beans, to tell everything, she humiliates him from behind the glass. Hey! You son of a bitch! And if I were to talk? Thief! Junkie! Murderer! Daniel flees.

Then an eighteen-year-old boy who begs him to let him pay later, who makes promises. Daniel says no. He'd like to help him, really, he's so ill at ease. But he's not the one who decides. He apologizes. The boy is thin, pale, sickly. He's shaking. He can't take it anymore. He dares not look at the sky. The angels are taunting him from up there. He's all alone, frail, on this hard earth, in the cold. And Daniel is moved to tears. He stands his ground. No, no, I can't, sorry, a thousand times no, no. The other insists, abject, half dead. Daniel looks at his face. He won't last long. Daniel knows it. He sees that... he's about to give in. Oh well, just a bit, hardly anything – Daniel pays out of his own pocket. He goes away. And leaves the boy under the falling snow.

Daniel moves on. An old madam converted to good works. She offers him cake and coffee. She simpers a little, my dear Daniel, what's become of you, you should drop in more often! She murmurs a few obscenities. Daniel blushes. He'd like to escape, get up and leave. He doesn't have the will power. The madam plants herself in front of him, spreads her thighs, fan-like, her gluey sex, its flaccid lips, slack, the smell! Daniel can take no more. From red, he turns white. She calls to him! Daniel, Daniel, come here! She mewls. He covers his face. Daniel! Daniel! Come! She grabs a candle, a big red one meant for Mass. Daniel! Daniel! Daniel rises. That is, something in him rises up, a feeling that's beyond him, exceeds him, fear and disgust together, he grabs the money off the table, and flees.

*

But it's when he arrives at old Pottier's, where he has an appointment with the man's son Jean, that he's overcome with fear. A genuine terror. Visceral. The fear of a hunted animal. A police car is parked in front of the house. Daniel sees shadows moving around behind the windows. A uniform. He slows. He stops. He doesn't know what to do. Should he stay? Should he go? How not to attract attention. Everything's reeling around him already, handcuffs, bars, the judge's ugly face like a cartoon, with the white wig and the gavel, the shame, his mother's sad gaze, his dry throat, what will they do with him?

Then Jean comes out of the house and goes to his car. Daniel is sweating, unsteady. He asks quietly what's going on, his voice halting. "It's nothing. The old man hanged himself." Ah. "The cops are leaving. They're just waiting for the ambulance. They don't know anything. Not a thing." Daniel is reassured. If the old man's hanged himself... Yes, of course the cops would be there. Jean tells him he'll have to come by the next day. Forget about today. There's nothing to be done when there are cops and a hanged man in the house. Daniel leaves. He doesn't know where he's at or what he wants. He goes home, his hands on the steering wheel, shaking.

*

His house is a hovel in the midst of a scrapyard. The first room you see when you go in is empty, no furniture.

There are two ways into the kitchen – one through the door, the other through a hole in the wall. A pail full of the water that drips from the ceiling, an echoing plink plink plink. Two small children, his, are playing on the floor with plastic cars. He enters without saying a word. It's cold. There's no power. His mother is in the corner looking at him, humming to herself. He waves to her and goes upstairs to his room.

There, he thinks to himself that he'd like to stop, to end his deliveries. He doesn't want to do it anymore, but how to go about it? Because it's Odette who decides. She has the say. Go on, Daniel, keep at it. You don't want to stop. It's a slippery slope for you either way. Life itself guarantees it. He'd like to slam on the brakes, to say no, no Odette, it's over. I'm taking you away and there'll be no more dealing. Come. We'll go away. Someplace warm, where the air is mild! But he won't tell her that. Would he ever dare? Can he even say it to himself?

*

I've pushed open the doors of houses. I've asked to see. To be told things. Indifference, say the sociologists, is the plague of our day. We hardly ever see another individual when he is suffering, when he cries out. We're shut up inside ourselves. And the thinkers give reasons. They have explanations. Mechanical ones. They say there's such a thing as "societal gears." And maybe there are.

But Odette and Daniel, don't they have to scale their own wall before peering down into someone else's garden? That daunting wall looming up between the world and themselves. Hemming them in. Throwing them back on themselves. And when they manage to hoist themselves to the top, it's only to get a peek, just barely, arms strained, both feet dangling in the air. They see the neighbour's garden. Of course, it's ugly. Of course, it's hideous. Perhaps they see that? They want to do something? Shout out some advice? Toss down a silver dollar? But what they're thinking, uncomfortable as they are, is that their muscles ache, that there's a cramp creeping in – and that they're weary from having climbed so high. They let go. They fall. Forget what they've seen. They only feel a self-inflicted sprain. Odette holds her head in both hands. Daniel too. They brood over their love. Odette thinks that prison has done her in, that her husband died after an attack from the antlers of a moose. Daniel thinks of Odette, and that he has to sell drugs to finance his trial. And may the neighbour's house go up in flames. All they will see is smoke in the distance.

*

Daniel called Odette the other day, his heart in his mouth. He told her that he wanted to stop. Oh, not seeing her! Not that! He told her that they'd keep seeing each other, absolutely. She shouldn't worry. But the trafficking, he couldn't do that anymore, his mother must know about it, that worried him, and he felt soiled, really soiled. He said he had to stop, now. Please... And then he got all confused... "I love you," that's what rose up his neck towards his lips. And also "come," he was going to take her far away, all of that a rasp in his throat, yet nothing, nothing at all – in the end, only silence.

"It's too late."

So he said nothing. For a few seconds he remained mute. And then he simply said yes. Odette hung up. Daniel too. Yes. I'll do it. Yes. He knew. That he'd gone too far. Only he needed to hear it said. By her. To be

spurred on by his fate. To be certain that he'd go all the
way. One night he'd taken a step too far. The one that
closes all the doors. And leaves you outside, alone, in the
cold. You have to move on. He'll have to move on for a
long time still.

*

It's a trial that has put Daniel up against the wall, a trial
that requires money, more money than he can earn from
his snow removal. Daniel is caught up in a trial involving
two guys that came one morning, when he was working
in a quarry a few kilometres away. They'd mocked him
at first, saying he was ugly and really dumb. An idiot.
A failure. Daniel took it. He was just a bit embarrassed...
ashamed. He went red in the face and didn't know what
to say. Then the two guys approached him. Threatening. One said he would kill him. The other said that he
would kill him, then he'd kill his mother. And Daniel
got mad. He threw himself on the second, broke his jaw,
then on the first one too, who'd backed off, and broke
his arm. He finished them off on the ground. In the gut.
The face. The two of them had trouble getting up. One
was blind for ten kilometres on the way back. And they
lodged a complaint. Daniel would certainly lose his trial.
Because he knew how to fight. But not how to defend
himself.

So, he asked Odette, who knew a little (he
cleared her snow). She was persuasive, had the get-
up-and-go that he lacked, she told him straight out
that he would lose his trial, that he'd owe money, that
he'd go to jail if he couldn't pay. He was frightened.
Swore that he'd done nothing. She made him understand that that didn't make any difference, that he'd

go to prison. So of course, Daniel asked how he could get the money. Odette told him, "Work for me, it's not a big deal, it's not demanding, it's almost legal: take care of the deliveries." It was a perfect opportunity for her. His trafficking was starting to get around, in the village, elsewhere, there were rumours... A dimwit like Daniel, who needed money, who was used to covering the region to clear the snow, who knew everybody, whom everyone knew, a dimwit like him would be perfect for her. Daniel agreed, thanking her. But also said that he was ashamed, that it would cause pain to his mother, that he couldn't lie to her and that she would guess everything. Odette reassured him: "It's not for long, just until the trial." That it wouldn't last.

But the trial has still not taken place. And the lie has settled in. The shame as well. He does Odette's errands. Word gets around. In a small village nothing is secret. What's buried comes to the surface. Before, he was thought of as an honest imbecile. Now, in the eyes of the world, he's just dishonest scum. People are afraid of him, avoid him. At the supermarket they lower their eyes when they see him – because he's "like that" – they turn their backs when he comes by. Daniel feels it all. He'd like to say something, apologize, make people understand. Sometimes you see him open his mouth, make a gesture – and then his hand drops, he says nothing. He never knows how to complete a gesture, or a word. Any kind of expression is beyond him.

He accepted the job, at first, out of necessity. And then when he knew Odette better, he accepted because Odette asked him. As simple as that. She was seductive, even if she was too thin. She knew how to command, she talked to him sternly, or sometimes softly to reassure him. He needed someone to say those things. That he was not the failure everyone said. That people were interested in him. Odette knew how to handle him. Sometimes she pressed his arm or whispered sweet nothings in his ear. Simple things. That didn't commit her. But still made Daniel feel that perhaps all was not lost. That cast light on his thoughts, offering a glimmer of hope. And Daniel moved on, his eyes on that light. He truly believed in it.

What they lack, in the end, is the stamina, the ardour, the stature that sets a man on a mountain top. They are those for whom cadence has replaced rhythm.

They're on their way down. It's a slippery slope. I'd like to reach out a hand, to stop them at the ledge so they don't plunge... I call them, hands cupping my mouth, from the depths of winter. But the gusts are so strong. I grope, I lose them, another blast – blood is running from my eyes. Odette! Odette! Answer me! Daniel! Where have they vanished to? Into what chasm? Buried by what avalanche? Suddenly winter lets up briefly, and I see them, but God! They're so far, small, huddling in the storm, I cry out, I call to them. They hear nothing. No one. No one hears them. And the clouds come back, as I watch – and I see nothing more. Where are they? Where will they fall? I glimpse the worst, I say it aloud. I have my reasons. You don't believe me? You think I'm being fatalistic? Look for yourself! What can you do? "In their place," you say, "I wouldn't do that." But you *are* in their place. You'll be there soon! I promise. I see you ending up with the rope around your neck, the gun in your fist. There are no other options.

Often, we dither endlessly over nonsense, we ingest antidotes, we treat ourselves to vacations, pile on "fine pleasures." The hedonism of our time. And yet eating and growing fat won't prevent us, one fine day, from making the cold calculation that it's not enough. That we want something else. That we want to be other. And the questioning begins. The educated will read philosophy, others will consult specialists. And when in the end they run out of options and admit that they will never be what they'd have wished to be, they go to extremes. All that is the tragedy of not living up to one's dreams. Ever since he's been in love, Daniel has hated himself. He doesn't want Odette to love him, to fall in love with him as if giving alms – he wants to be *the one* whom Odette loves. To be alchemically transformed into the man Odette adores.

And Odette dreams of being Jean's wife.

*

Odette looks out the window, through the slats of the blinds. There are cops at old man Pottier's. She thinks at once that Jean must have been busted. It's likely. To be expected. And she smiles. Because the true face of love smiles when those you love are unhappy. Odette imagines Jean in his cell – hers, all hers, dependent, alone in the world. The others will leave. She will stay. And he will be grateful. They're far away, I'm nearby, you are mine. The heart doesn't work any other way. Odette makes castles in the air for a few moments, has visions, feels good. She plans her visits, she'll go on the fifteenth of the month, yes, that's good, half-way, and also how she'll wear her hair, what dress, which perfume, details. The story seems already set down. Jean is mine!

No doubt he won't be released just like that. It could take two years. Two years, that's huge! Twenty-four visits! More if he marries her. Nothing moves. The cop's car is parked, and nothing moves. What are they talking about? She waits to see them come out from one minute to the next. Jean with his hands behind his back, handcuffed, and she who will appear and tell him not to worry, telling him in a few seconds that she'll be there for him. But they don't come out. Odette is confused. What's going on?

The pictures fly by. When she met him, Jean was living with his parents. He'd got out of prison for the Christmas holidays. They'd eaten turkey together. Surrounded by the decorations. The manger. The coloured lights. A holly branch. By the time dessert was served, everyone was drunk. And she and Jean had sex in a car, his brother's Camaro. He smelled of alcohol. As did she. It was brutal. And he said to her, "Odette, Odette, I fuck better than your old man, I'm as good as him, a hell of a lot better even, 'cause he's cold and I'm alive." Jean said that, and he was thinking about all of Odette's cash. That she'd inherited. And she believed him. Her life had been bitter enough for her to sweeten it with hope. This young guy was so honest! Oh, she didn't really see him! Now, of course, she does. She's got his number, he was just selling her wind. But she'd already put money on the table, her heart above all. She was one step too deep in love. With this big lunk she couldn't get along without. And he couldn't give a damn. And still doesn't. Except that today she still can't do without him. She's taken a fall. And never should have. Finish the turkey and take to your heels! Disappear! Get away from the dark eyes of this tall Jean. Her strength has failed her. She misses him still. If only she could... She's furious. "If I were somebody," she thinks, "he'd love me!" She doesn't see that Jean won't love her under any circumstances. That it's not in his nature. That he doesn't like people who don't bring him cash. That if Odette had a million, he'd steal it, and be off like a shot. He would steal her glory, her fortune. He'd suck the lifeblood out of her, then disappear. Jean is a loner, a cutthroat hermit for whom others are only good for his own survival. To keep him in orbit.

*

When the police ring, Odette takes the time to look at herself in the mirror, to tuck away a lock of hair, to smile to herself. To adorn her mask. And its attendant dignity. She graciously opens the door. "Good day, Sergeant!" She can see on his face that this is not a matter for hand-cuffs. Not for Jean. Nor even for her. She frowns. He confirms it. Old Pottier has hanged himself. "That's so sad." A few questions. For the form. The report. "Have a good day, Madame." "You too."

CHAPTER 3

When Jean Pottier found his father that morning, he first searched his pockets. The old man's tongue was hanging out, his eyes were enormous, his face black. Jean took his gold watch and a twenty-dollar bill. He then went to the living room sideboard. He didn't have the key. He would have forced it, but the police would be coming, then his brothers and sisters, it would be noticed. And if he became a suspect? If they said he was the one who'd hung him up? When he'd done nothing? That would be really stupid... So much for the sideboard. And then... it would be better like this, more dignified. His conscience fell back on that fact. He went to the bar for a sip of whisky. Should he call the police? Of course. But Daniel was coming with the cocaine. So? If the cops were there, Daniel would take off for sure, and if they weren't, he would tell him to leave. That was clear. There didn't seem to be any risk. All things considered. The way things added up. So, he called the police. It would take them two good hours to get there, what with the storm. He had to wait, and he had the time. He thought again about it all, his old father. And he felt sad.

*

I'd never much liked Jean. We'd had run-ins. He was like the bad guy in movies, but with something missing; there was something laughable about him, a hint of weakness. His mischief was all for nothing in the Quebec north, in the forest, in Notre-Dame-de-la-Merci, in envelopes of coke. Though he was seen as a big bandit, a murderer, he was really just an abject drunk, a bit of a druggie who battered women. He didn't have the passion for a major crime, or the ambition. He didn't have enough red blood in his veins. Sometimes he worked out a plan. Checked out the terrain. Maybe even took some notes. But his laziness caught up with him, along with the fog – and he went back to lie down again.

Way back when he was a kid, he'd had big ideas. For him, a tree house reached to the sky. He was going to be a leader of men. There were a few holdups, too, supermarkets, the Toys "R" Us in the city. But he always ended up doing what the other kids did. No more, no less. His thoughts carried him away. But his behaviour was totally ordinary.

His adolescence was ordinary too. He jerked off a lot. Drank. Did drugs. He listened to Black Sabbath and the pioneers of British Heavy Metal, even scratched out a few chords. He had it off with girls in beat-up cars. Normal stuff, like everybody else. All around, over hundreds of kilometres, destinies just like his were working themselves out, painfully, between two huffs of hash. His adolescent dreams were no different from those of the others. Go into town, hauling a guitar. Be discovered, have meaning, learn despite yourself that you're a genius, and then believe in it enough to make others believe it too. Cut a disc. The dreams take over when you're with your buds. And when the buds go away, the dreams last a bit longer. Sometimes they eat away at you. Gnaw.

It's when he hurt a woman for the first time, really, in the heart and in the face, that Jean became aware of his power, of the fact that he was, himself, powerful – and that the others were not. And so, he made himself scary. Cultivated a mask. Became cold and brutal. Calm on the surface, but ready to pounce. He made sure that everybody knew. The grandmothers in the area were afraid. The neighbours said that he was bad news and forbade their children to talk to him. Kids his age began to avoid him. And he felt good about it. It was said that one day the cops would pick him up for something serious. Meanwhile, he was a threat. And Jean played the role. He still does. But his character lacks substance. At first, he'd wanted to lead a gang, to be the first in line of the guys nearby, in a cartel, but it all seemed like too much trouble, and risky as well. He wanted to pull off a big heist at the Caisse Desjardins, but again he lacked the nerve, or maybe just the strength. Then he bashed in a guy's face, badly, and the guy didn't make a complaint. So, he was feared a bit more. His big achievement was having been able, at the age of twenty-two, to pass himself off as a tough. It was no big deal. From here, it can even seem a bit ridiculous. But when you feel tough in a little village, there's no comparing. And the people around you, they've got nothing to compare you with either, so they're ready to believe that you're invincible. That's the key to local glory.

*

When Daniel comes down to the living room, his mother motions him, quietly, to come to her, don't be afraid.

He goes over slowly, not at all reassured, like a child who has done something wrong, trembling, swallowing tears. He's sure she knows. He wants to open his mouth, to say something. She tells him that there's no point, that she knows everything. So, Daniel protests. It's not true! It's all lies. And then the tears spring to his eyes. He knows he won't get away with this. He makes no more denials. Rather, he gets confused. It's not for long. It's for the trial. He swears it. It won't last. She tells him that it doesn't matter, she doesn't care if it's for the trial or something else, never mind, she, his mother, wants him to stop. Daniel doesn't reply. Only weeps.

Then she talks about Odette, because she knows perfectly well what's going on, who was able to persuade her son, and how. She hates her. For what she's doing to her son, and also for the place she has taken in Daniel's heart. Hearing her name, "Odette," Daniel explodes, vents his suppressed rage. He straightens up. His voice gains strength. He's not a child anymore. He tells her that it's none of her business, who does she think she is? He yells. He threatens. Maybe he believes what he's saying? Maybe at this moment he really wants to hurt her? He moves towards his mother, threatening; he wants to assert himself, like his father when he was alive, lashing with his belt. But the old lady faces up to him. She's not afraid. She'd been afraid of her husband. She fears nothing from her son. He cries again that it's not true, they're lies! Lies! And then he turns around. Picks up his coat and leaves the house; the door slams. His mother stays back in the shadows, says not a word.

Outside, he tries to catch his breath. Tears run down his cheeks and freeze on his chin. "But since it's too late? Since it's too late?" he repeats under his breath.

"Since it's too late." He loses himself in the storm. Flakes in his eyes. On his face. Everything around him disappears. He thinks he's lost, forgotten. "That's just fine!" he thinks. Then it all scares him and his head spins. So, he goes into his garage, turns the key, and lights a cigarette – and he stays there, at his workbench, head in his hands. He wishes he could break free. Kick his way out. Stop. Start again. But Odette is right. He'll carry on to the end.

*

Daniel takes his tools. Dismantles the motor in front of him. He's promised it to Bélanger for Friday. It has to be finished. At first, he can't concentrate, the screwdriver slips, he doesn't know what to do. And then, little by little, he remembers. The feeling comes back. The smell of oil calms him. The grime. It's restful, familiar. The vise that clamps his heart loosens. He works. He'll work until nightfall. His cigarette pack on the workbench, his lighter, in the cold. In the dark and the cold. And silence. Once in a while, perhaps, he'd like to say something. But that something doesn't take shape. The words don't come. If he talks it's to say nothing, and what is speech anyway? All the words that matter get away from him.

*

Brought up more or less freely in the Quebec woods, I would have scoffed at any guy who told me that in his opinion freedom didn't exist. It would have struck me as ridiculous, and I'd have thought he was crazy. And so I never believed in Fate. I still don't. Anyone who says that everything is predetermined by I don't know what Eye is full of it and and their ideas don't hold water. It's all nonsense and a way to make yourself feel that everything is where it belongs. That if you're not free, you're genuine. That's better. You don't owe anyone anything. The idea that Man is guided by the Powers has always struck me as phony.

Yet the idea made its way. But in the manner of Odette. Without metaphysics. Without a veiled power to guide the hand of man. My determinism became purely physical. It was all a connective web. And I thought it was terrible.

I had a lengthy conversation with myself. Gave myself shit. What, how can you believe such a thing? You can see perfectly well that you're free! Don't be ridiculous! It's obvious! I argued with myself, saying that I could see clearly that the earth was flat, yet upon reflection that didn't hold water... Still, I brooded for a long time. At the end my head was all in a fog... I didn't know any more... Today I still don't know... I waver... I'm obsessed.

One night a guy told me that I was lucky to be able to write, that not everyone could do it, and that in fact it was kind of rare. So, I went on the attack. A child, on the run. My old ideals. I replied that it was not a matter of luck, and that everyone could express himself in one way or another. And he said no. And I said yes. Yes, everyone is free to pick up a pen or a microphone, to make a noise, make art, to emerge from silence. He denied it. He didn't think the world was free. He didn't believe men were free. I found his ideas cynical. That wasn't what I believed. And then I thought some more. It seemed to me, my head spinning, that free will is never evident. In theory, it's far from being certain. It's a wager you make, that's all.

And I realized that this man was being in no way cynical. On the contrary, that his denial of free will is what enabled him to express his tenderness. That he was full of love and compassion for mankind, and there was nothing cynical about it. This same tenderness is what inspired me one day when, walking near a public park, I saw a big man all in black saying to the children playing there that he was covered with scabs, that it was itchy under his scrotum, and that he'd show it to them if they wanted. To which the children were about to reply that yes, they wanted to, not knowing what the big man was talking about, but being curious all the same. That same tenderness is what made me take the man by the shoulders, firmly, without violence, and lead him out of the park and onto the sidewalk, leaving him to his fantasies, and his itch. Another man, perhaps, more enlightened than me, might have punched out one of his eyes, handed him over to the cops, then gone back to the children to teach them a lesson. He would have told them that you have to deserve to be treated well, that they'd seen an instance of a black sheep who had, by his own fault, strayed from good behaviour, and had to, by "working on himself," right his ship and behave better. And that you must never accept candy from anyone or look at anyone's penis. My own heart was full of tenderness for the man whose impulses were so tenacious, so monstrously clear. I had seen at once, when he was no more than a silhouette, that he was far more sad than dangerous. And it's because I know what sad men do, that I approached him. And it's because I love them that I didn't turn him in to the police.

*

Jean knocks at the door. Odette shudders. She'd of course seen him coming up the steps. He doesn't seem sad. Maybe he's going to boast. She'd like to take him in her arms. Jean enters without saying a word and goes straight to the living room. Odette shuts the door and checks to see if anyone has observed them. Nobody. Jean pours himself a drink. Odette looks at him, inspects him, seeks hints of sadness or despair, a wound to dress – something to give her a clue. But Jean sips his drink as usual, nothing more, nothing less. He seems to be thinking of something else, something far away. The silence drags on. Odette tries to break it. She coughs, shifts an object. Jean says nothing. Makes no moves other than those required to take a drink. Odette can bear it no longer. She takes a chance. "How are you feeling?" Adding that she is very sorry. She'd like to talk more about death, but the only death she's known is her husband's, and she'd rather leave that alone. Jean looks her in the eyes. Gives her an unpleasant smile. Tension. Odette trembles. He can see it. Her frozen smile. And then he laughs, softly at first, a kind of chuckle, and then openly. "But I'm fine, Odette dear! I'm really fine. And I haven't been left empty- handed!" And he raises his arm, the gold watch is there on his wrist. Odette understands. She's seen that watch before. "You see, I've worn it for you. Do you like it? It's gold, come and look at it, come here." She goes closer. Mechanically. Because he's told her to. "So, do you like it?" Odette is facing him. She doesn't reply. "I asked you, do you like it?" Finally, she says, very softly, that she does. She tries to pull herself together. What is this man doing in her living room? Had she even asked him in? No, she doesn't like him. She's not even afraid of him. She doesn't love him. And so? She goes closer, resolute, sure of herself, then stares at him in turn. "What are you doing here?" He says he's come for the cocaine, since Daniel couldn't stop by. She loses her temper. She'd told him not to come, it was too dangerous, they were being watched. "Come on! What with the old man, they've got other things on their minds. Don't get so worked up, Odette dear, don't get so upset. Nobody knows. And really, nobody cares." She's furious. "You don't know anything! No! You don't know a thing!" Jean laughs. She's still angry. He should go. She wants him to go. "Tomorrow Daniel will come to see you, he'll bring you the stock."

"I want it now."

Odette is ready to explode, shout, cry... But she controls herself.

"Daniel will come to see you tomorrow."

Jean gets up, slowly, menacingly. He grabs Odette by the throat and pushes her against the wall, knocks over her figurines. He whispers into her face:

"Now."

Jean smells of alcohol. Odette's not afraid, she's wounded; she's ashamed. She doesn't want tears. She doesn't cry out. Jean lets her go and takes the drugs. "I'll come back with the money." He leaves. Odette brings her hand to her throat, then to her heart because that's where it hurts. She picks up a figurine, hurls it to the floor. Hurls the bottle and Jean's glass against the wall.

*

There are long evenings when we drink a lot. When we talk a blue streak. About what you'd call "Fate," which is often a kind of Providence, and which for me is a web of connections. For others, the idea is comforting. For me, it's disturbing. "You have to like things as they are," they say. But I don't think of things as they are. I think of them as I'd like them to be. Whence my uneasiness. Whence my wrenching unhappiness. I think of Odette. I think of Daniel, who wants to be the one whom Odette adores. And so? And so, there is no place in the world for free men and for men of destiny – in terms of whether they are reconciled with their own lives, or not. Either all men are free, or all is foreordained for them.

*

The ambulance has come to remove the body. Jean has sat back down at the bar. He's drinking while he waits for his brother, who has told him that he's on his way. Charles seemed shattered. His voice broke, his sentences went nowhere. Jean is a bit sad too, but sad like when you're surrounded by a fog, when the weather is bad. The background is grey, that's all. And it's on this grey background that he continues to inscribe his projects, Mexico, where he wants to go, Sabrina, the beautiful Sabrina, whom he'll take with him, or whom he'll go to meet, whom he'll marry perhaps – depending on how he feels. And other things too, his own trafficking, his little business. When Charles arrives, he'll know how to put on a face, to don a mask. For his future is before him now – and no shadow is going to be cast upon it. He's thinking of his father's legacy. Did the old man have money? Most likely. A lot? He couldn't say. The father was always wary of the son. "For sure there'll be enough for a meal." And he realizes that he's hungry. He opens the fridge. The old man tended to let everything rot. It smells strong, like in the bedroom upstairs, but he really is hungry.

*

Daniel is sitting in the garage, working on his motor. He hears the door open. The wind rushes into the room. He turns around, fearful. It's his daughter. With a doll broken in two, decapitated. She asks if he can glue it back together. He smiles. Takes the toy in his hands, delicately. He promises to do what he can. She can come and get it later. He waits. She's silent. "And... And grandma?" Grandma said she's waiting for him. The soup is ready. Tonight's supper will be cold because there's no electricity, so it can wait. Whenever he wants. Daniel says he'll finish with the motor, he'll glue the doll, and he'll be there – relieved that the quarrel with his mother has ended like the others, like before, like always.

When he enters the house, nothing has changed. His children are playing on the floor and his mother is sitting in her corner, in the shadows. The candlelight adds warmth to the scene. That comforts him. He goes towards her. She asks if his work has gone well. He says yes and goes to sit at the table. His mother joins him. The children. She talks to him about the neighbour, Madame Simard, who dropped in for news. And also, for what's being said about the new mayor. What she heard last week about the Ouellette children. About him, about their quarrel, not a word, not even an allusion. Nor about Odette, or drugs, or anyone. Daniel eats slowly. He listens. Doesn't speak. He knows that she knows, that she hasn't forgotten. He feels very strongly that this is all a masquerade. But he lacks the courage to admit it honestly to himself, or even to break the silence, stop the show. On the contrary, he lapses into it. He's hungry. He eats. His mother goes on reciting stories, banalities, gossip, rolling out the nonsense in which she's swaddling him. The children listen too, vaguely conscious of what's going on. And then, fatally, a stumble. What did she say? Could she have mentioned Lac-en-Croix, or talked about Jean, who knows? Her edifice teeters, crumbles all at once. Daniel's hands shake. He's in a cold sweat. "I'll make you some tea." His mother rises and goes to the kitchen. His daughter says Papa, Papa, are you all right? Are you sick? He doesn't hear. He's over-come. He doesn't know. His mother comes back with the tea. "Drink, Daniel, forget it, drink, don't worry." "Drink, Papa, drink." Daniel doesn't drink. He does nothing. He's like his shadow in the sun, that slips away from him, melts away. "Drink, Daniel, I beg you, drink." At last he comes back to himself, barely, ever so slightly. He holds the cup by its handle. Brings the cup to his lips. Everything is shaking. His mother takes his hand. His two children huddle around him, at his knees. Papa, papa. Drink, Dan-iel, drink. One more swallow, colours come back to him. Slowly. Quietly. Along with the tea. Life. Another swallow. He can feel again. He can think, a little. There are things that caress his skin. His mother smiles. The children have understood. He looks around him. He opens up a bit more. He's at home. "Come, Daniel, finish your supper, don't worry. You'll sleep afterwards. Tonight, you'll sleep. Tomorrow things will be better." And motherly love casts its spell over him once again. He lies down on the couch. His mother's web all around, rocking him, casting a spell over his memories, and he sleeps.

*

But what if they're right? The silent ones. Perhaps the whole truth is theirs as they submit to their tragedy, as they adjust to it. Maybe the anonymous ones are, after all, the genuine representatives of our race. And the sub-lime poets, the glorious ones, are the liars. The realist painters are not those we think. The true painter is at one with his paint.

*

Charles climbs the steps with great dignity, his dark coat dusted with a few flakes, his eyes red. He is a doctor. He works with the insane. With the dead also, but as statistics in a register. The death of one of his own, of his father, is not just something recorded – this he is not used to. Jean comes to meet him, head bowed. He embraces him. "My poor brother!" They meet, they embrace – they forget their little wars. "How sad! Dear God! Our father! Who'd have believed it! Dear God! How sad!" Jean plays his role. He plays it well. "Then it's you who ... found him?" Jean confirms it. Did he leave a note? No, nothing. Silence. It's incomprehensible. Charles, the brain doctor, says it: it makes no sense. What to do, when it makes no sense? Keep on going, of course. Charles gropes around, blindly. He has opened men up and cast his eyes from top to bottom. But today he thinks he must have forgotten something. Why is the old man's carcass so dear to him? Why does he realize that it was part of him, as well? Why does he feel naked, dispossessed? Maybe there is something more than the sum of what we were offered in our schoolbooks? Charles trembles. His shoulders are laden with a heavy burden. He's hunched over, and what else? Another ghost? Lost, in the storm and to himself, where does this complaint come from, and this weight, this chill – how is it that the old man still has him by the throat? He stops at the door. Jean turns. "You feel sick?" Charles says no, it's all right, not really but I'll be okay, I'm fine." They go inside. "A drink, to pick us up?" Charles accepts. Face to face, the two brothers give each other courage, colour – they get their blood circulating. They exchange news. Jean invents something. A return to the straight and narrow. "Don't worry about me." Then they talk about their childhood, the past, their parents, the shadow of their father that hovers over them, implacable. Sometimes Charles interrupts. Tears come to his eyes. The ghost brushing against him. And Jean too, honestly, doesn't feel that well... He has fits of trembling. And then he recovers. He can recover quickly. The mask hardens, in his eyes there is a thickening... How did it happen? What did the police say? The details. Did the neighbours hear anything? The ambulance? And the funeral? What should we do? And then they get to it slowly... The inheritance? The money? The sister, the brother. They have to share. "Equally," Jean insists. Four equal parts. He says nothing about the watch, of course. Which lies in the bottom of his jacket pocket. Nothing about the sideboard either. He only talks about what the other knows. The brothers sigh... Charles says that they'll see about it all later, it's still too fresh, too painful,,,,,. "Of course," Jean says, "let's wait. There's no hurry. Between brothers and sisters..." Only the ceremony is urgent. What day? They agree on Friday. Yes, sure, that's fine, Friday.

When Charles has left Jean comes back from the garage with a crowbar. He pries open the door of the sideboard. Three thousand dollars and porn mags. He saw nothing of his brother's distress. Of his suffering. He saw only his own interests.

*

A few years ago, Odette had wanted to be mayor. To be first lady of the village. She started to campaign, very seriously and at great expense. First, she put up posters with her face on them, and a powerful slogan, "All with me." The photographer had done his job. She was almost beautiful. Except for the eye sockets a bit too deep, and the prominent cheekbones. Odette then organized gatherings, with implausible speeches about violence to women, the education of young people, and above all, drugs, which were a plague, one that she'd wipe out, fast. The village was receptive. Everywhere they said that she was elegant and eloquent. There were of course a few skeptics and no lack of rumours. Daniel's mother said out loud that she was phony, all wind, just putting on an act. Another, Madame Boisvert, asserted that she had lovers. That she knew things she couldn't say. Only allusions, winks. Others had doubts. Still, in general people were impressed, and halfway through the campaign it was already conceded that she would be taking her place in the mayor's office. Odette was confident. Her glory rang in her ears to the point that she didn't hear the grumbling, the spitting in the ditch, all the Madame Boisverts, the unbelievers. Her speeches ended up attracting people from all around, from beyond the village – Saint-Donat, Rawdon, even from Saint-Agathe, Saint-Côme. They assembled in the big hall with the orange chairs and the ugly stage, to hear Odette, poised, talk about everything that was wrong: the children, the violence, the drugs. Odette cherished those moments when she rose to speak and felt herself being borne away. When she felt important, more than that, when she felt herself growing – existing. Then, on stage, before beginning, she would half-close her eyes and look up towards the ceiling. It was her heaven. The sea-green fluorescents. And the applause.

But at her peak, the sky fell. Cops turned up at her place. "My escort!" But it was to arrest her. Cocaine. The judge laughed a little when he heard the story, even told her not to worry, it wasn't very serious – what an insult! Odette still raised her head, she looked him up and down, defied him, I confess everything, yes, everything – but there wasn't much to confess. The judge had told her so. She got six months and a fine. When she got out, there was of course no question of politics. Or the public. Or speeches. Her life's dream was ended.

*

Odette is still ranting. After the insult she cries out, her face contorted with rage. He'll pay, oh boy, I'll show him, that lousy piece of crap. What he stole from her. He'd be nothing without her. And her heart too, she's in tears, racked by palpitations. She lets fly whatever comes to hand – and it all bangs, wham, bam, a storm of earthenware, pots and pans, china. And the cries! That scar the throat! That exhaust it! That ring out in the tempest, that blot out even the wind, all her hatred, her love – all the blood that flows, exposing the silence. That ruptures it! Gashes it! I'll kill Jean! More things broken. She heaves a drawer full of metal buttons against the wall. She up-ends a low table with one blow. A hammer flies through a window. She retrieves it. Tosses it onto the couch, for later. And the outsize fury. The tragedienne's howls. She bleeds a little, a shard of glass in her hand. There's blood on her dress. She looks awful. Seeing the blood, she thinks that it's just the start, there will be a lot more – that the storm is only beginning.

*

Jean leaves his father's house, it's night. Nights in Quebec woods are dense and narrow and closed in on themselves: disturbing. Jean is on his feet in the night. At ease. He knows he's not in danger. That the danger is him. He raises his head and savours beneath the sky Odette's dread. He can feel the subterranean, nocturnal rippling of the drama that is brewing. He guesses that this night will open onto other nights, darker still – and that only he will escape unscathed.

*

As Jean is getting into his car, he hears steps behind him. He turns around. Odette's silhouette stands out against the night. Her eyes are shining. Her teeth. He feels her shivering from a chill that has nothing to do with the wind. "Odette, dear, to what do I owe the pleasure?" Odette doesn't answer. She comes closer. And suddenly, a cry! Odette pounds her fist into Jean's face. He staggers, groans. She takes out her hammer. And she strikes. Jean goes down.

Odette yells and strikes with all her might, with all the power long coiled up deep inside her, the rancour now unfurled into the dark night. And she kicks. Jean is being walloped. Cowering, humiliated, he's getting a drubbing! Odette beats him to her heart's content. He's bleeding. And shielding his face with his hands. Too dazed to get up. To grab the hammer. And knock Odette over. Shit! To be at her mercy like that. His mind is fogged. She strikes again. His vision is blurred.

And then... And then the blows are less relentless. More hesitant. Odette weakens. She still cries out, of course, shrieks that she hates him, die, die, but the blows? They don't lie. Jean sees it. He's almost lost consciousness, yet he feels that he's already won. Won again. He smiles. In the snow. His mouth bloody. His strength returns, he says to himself that after all it's only Odette, and it's always been only Odette. So, he gets up. And she, she trembles. She's afraid. She stops trying to hit him. She goes silent. Jean is facing her. He grabs her by the collar and pushes her into the snow. Odette slips. Falls. Jean picks up the hammer. He approaches Odette, lying in the snow. "What's going on, Odette dear?" And he laughs. Because all this pleases him. He knows Odette is afraid, and that she loves him and that others will be afraid and that they'll love him too. "I thought we liked each other?" She bursts into tears. "I'll kill you," she repeats, her voice broken, "I'll kill you, you'll see who I am, I'll kill you." "You'll kill me?" That's not true.

*

Jean has left. He looks at himself in the rear-view mirror. He's bleeding heavily, his nose, his upper lip, his left temple. He groans, furious at looking like that. His anger grows, he wants revenge, wants to turn the car around, get even with the bitch. He slams his fist onto the steering wheel. He brakes, he stops, ready to go back the way he came. After all, why not, finally, a real crime? Why not put flesh on all the rumours? Why not kill Odette? But just asking the question brings him to his senses. When you kill, you know why. He has no reason to kill Odette. Because he's stronger than she is and she knows it, everyone knows it. He'll get his revenge, of course. Out of spite. And also, because, not believing for a moment that Odette can well and truly kill him, he thinks that she could cause him harm. She's crazy enough to go and denounce him, and bring him down. What's he risking? Not much, he knows, a lot less than her. But all the same. He smiles.

He'll make the first move.

*

A question with no answer is not empty, and questions are never merely theoretical. You can recognize a knit brow. People have scoffed at the thinker's pose. The question goes further than the way it is posed. It goes far beyond. The question works its way into your marrow. It rips apart your dreams. Overwhelms your lightness of heart. A psychology magazine published a young girl's question: "What is the use of living?" And the woman responsible for the column replied with inadequate platitudes. What response could have been good enough? The girl has doubtless forgotten it. But what she doesn't forget is the burning question, and she persists and plays games with the answers. An open question is a question that bleeds.

In reading philosophy, it is not rare to think that the argument is brilliant, the reasoning impelling – you surrender to it nearly completely – but that all the same, something is missing. A tiny residue that prevents you from going along with it. You say that it must be right, logically, but you don't put faith in it. All angst derives from that residue.

CHAPTER 4

There is a church in Notre-Dame-de-la-Merci. A big church. Next door to the school. I've never been inside. I've never seen Jean there, nor Odette, nor Daniel. Odette says: "Let God take care of his business; I'll take care of mine." Daniel went to church with his mother when he was a child. But his father was jealous of the priest, of God too, so he said: "Don't go any more." She stopped going. Jean has never felt comfortable in a church.

And I don't go any more, just as I never go into schools or nurseries – because I've nothing to do there.

A century ago, the poor could pray. They were left alone. But the poor aren't dupes any more. They know that God doesn't exist. Because otherwise, they say, he wouldn't let all those things happen. Because it's fine to tell them that his decrees are hidden from them, but they don't believe it. They have the vague impression that everything is totally mixed up. They have a sense of the times they live in. But they don't know what to do with it. Should they rejoice? Should they weep? So, they forget. They blame heaven, as you do from a window that now gives onto nothing. But they end up missing the heaven's light. Its illumination. They don't understand themselves anymore. They don't know who they are. The things around them, when they think about it, have no meaning. Why are they wearing themselves out? Why are they still so restless? Why not do what they want? What's stopping them? Because they see clearly that they're being held back. That they're being restrained. Some push on ahead. They revolt. Others see fatality at work. An earthly weight. A fatality that's not written in any great book with letters of gold. But a fatality of dust and mud that they can never fathom. Others still know that in giving God his leave they have said no to reason. They make their own arrangements. They stop weighing things in the balance. They're indifferent. People say they're talking nonsense. And indeed, things no longer make sense to them.

*

Daniel is sitting in his room, on his bed. The power has come back, then disappeared, then come back for good. He's sitting under the fluorescent light. His room is shabby. The walls are cracked. It's cold. The wind is whistling. Downstairs, his mother is humming something, for herself, you'd think – but in fact it's for him, Daniel, so he won't be alone, so as to ward off the silence. His mother's song, drifting up, is a small bright glimmer that he treasures. But he also feels that it's not what he needs, that his heart is ardent, passionate, that it demands something more, that it wants her, Odette – and that his mother's love is only a pale imitation. Daniel wants more than his mother's music. He gets up abruptly, stands in the wan light. He will have her! Will he have her? He doesn't know. Yes. He will have her. He clenches his fists. Whatever it costs, didn't she promise that after the trial, if he behaved himself, they would leave together? Why not now? Immediately? Go and get Odette and spirit her away? She owes it to him. They'll be very happy. He imagines himself with Odette in a distant country, much like this one because his knowledge is limited, but with one crucial, though invisible feature: it's elsewhere. When they're together, what will they do? Maybe they'll be lying in a warm bed. Or they'll be in a store – people will see them together – or at work, he in his workshop, she in the living room, sitting in his mother's chair. Odette wouldn't have to sell drugs any more. Nor would Daniel. They'd never be afraid. And he'd no longer feel ashamed. He'd hold his head high. Meet people's eyes. Odette on his arm, smiling, like him. They ride together in Daniel's pick-up, the scoop raised, they are leaving for somewhere else, dear Lord! His heart is going to burst. The poor soul holds his sides. He falls back onto his bed, face down. And his mother's song down below, plaintive, tragic – so inadequate.

In the living room his mother is sitting, singing. The children are still playing, quietly, in a corner. The old woman has a feel for things. There was her husband, whose alcoholism she proudly endured until he went to his grave. She knows when a storm is brewing. And that this storm is about to destroy everything, to swell up, carry everything into the night. Her husband gave her a hard time until his death. He shut her up in a closet when he went whoring. Entire nights. The belt for the children – the hissing, the dull noise, the cries, and the tears. When he died, she still found the strength to mourn him. For herself, the strength to miss him. Her neighbours arrived smiling, to comfort her, telling her the future was going to brighten for her. She received them coldly, sad and pale, solemn in her sorrow.

And tonight, she feels that the storm is approaching. That it's only beginning. That the returning light is only the good Lord's ploy. That the night will be long. That it will take from her all she's been able to save. The old woman rises. Goes to the window. The snow has stopped falling. The wind is still blowing. She's not cold. Outside, in the neighbourhood, house lights are lit. The Simards are ready for Christmas. They have the most decorations. Every year they buy two hundred more bulbs. They say that it's for their grandchildren who are coming on vacation. So they'll feel welcomed. The big gifts are under the fir tree their grandfather brought in from the forest a few days early. So, there will be no false note. So, everything will be perfect. And the children think it's fine. Their grandparents too. Together, they're all fine. On Christmas Eve the grandfather gets dressed up. The grandmother is cooking. And the whole little household is filled with laughter. Its joy flows out onto the doorsteps for others.

Daniel's mother thinks about it all with sadness, but without bitterness. "When you can't, you can't, that's all." She looks at her grandchildren, sickly, thin, born by chance to one woman, then another. Both took off, leaving the children behind. "When you can't, you can't." Best not to think about it.

*

There's always one dream that contains all the others. When I was a child, one of my friends talked to me about China. He wanted to live in China. Everything he dreamed about took place in China. He learned as much about it as he could. His mother would tell him:

"Get up, talk to us about China." He got up, took his bag, and pulled out magazines, newspapers, and an exercise book into which he had glued his press clippings. That was his dream.

Jean had his own dream. I said that he saw himself as lord of the world, and that's true. He didn't see himself playing that part just anywhere. Ever since his uncle had brought him a poster from Mexico, he'd wanted to go there. It was there that he dreamed of being, of being strong, of reigning. He wasn't as scrupulous as my friend of course, with his clippings about China. But he asked his uncle to tell him about Mexico. He listened to him. He asked questions. And he went to lie down on his bed, closed his eyes, told himself it was certain that one day he would go to Mexico. When he met Sabrina, he wanted to take her there. She said no. He beat her. She left him. Then he got horny, he wanted to screw her again. And they reconciled. Jean doesn't love her. Sabrina doesn't love Jean. But in the end, he persuaded her to go to Mexico. Jean thinks that with his father's money, he'll be able to leave. He also thinks that before he leaves, he will denounce Odette.

*

Daniel's mother never had great hopes for her son. She did not dream of him having an impressive career or of winning the lottery. "When you can't, you can't." We're not the kind to allow ourselves to dream. Dreaming is good for others, for people who win, who succeed, but we're going nowhere and we're alone – we don't dream. She knows you can die from hope. She knows where it gets you. So, she lowers her eyes and looks at the ground. Because the ground doesn't lie.

She never told Daniel to look to the future. She never told him that he had to succeed. They're not happy where they are, but they know that they won't be happy anywhere else either. And so, they're resigned. The ceiling leaks and the walls are mouldy. They're right. Happiness is too high up and their legs are too weak. "When you can't, you can't." They don't have the strength, that's all there is to it.

Daniel's love for Odette seems to his mother a dangerous urge, a revolt. She'd like to tell him to forget it. To lower his sights. Not to aim so high. So he won't slide down from the precipice. She knows that Odette is not for him, never will be. So it would be best for him to buckle down. To keep on working, every morning, very early in winter, later in summer. Look at women? Maybe. Of course. But not Odette. He mustn't love her, because it's impossible. He should resign himself. Resign yourself, Daniel. Your shifting sands are worth more than a darkened sky.

*

So, there's no more God or master, no hope either. And some men understood that suffering was useful. That it could bring significant benefits. So, the masters returned. They blocked off the heavens with cells of slaves. They dressed them up and called them "sir". Told them that they had to live but to think little – that they ought to have only small thoughts. Told them that they could believe, but only in the short term. That the weather will be fine. That you will climax like never before. You'll win the jackpot. So, men began to believe again. Even to believe at top speed. Far more than before. Inflation set in. And their claims became worthless.

Because the new masters do not have the good Lord's powers. Eternity is lacking. And thunder in the fist. Lights alone are not enough. Neither is artifice. Their canned promises. They offer their goods. But of what use are their goods to me? Comfort. A change. But that's not sufficient. We eat, we sleep – finally we wake. And when we wake, we have to have strong nerves. Not too much of a yen for the precipice. You have to be able to begin again. Some do. Others don't have the strength. They stop.

*

Jean rings at Daniel's door. His mother opens it. She's afraid. The look on his face . "What's he doing here?" She knows that his being there does not bode well. She knows him by reputation, and also for having baby-sat him when he was a child. If he's here it's because he has an idea, and that can only be bad. She knows the rumours making the rounds. She knows the person he beat so badly, who didn't dare lodge a complaint. She knows that he's fooling around with Odette, at Lac-en-Croix. She also knows the pain it must be causing Daniel. Seeing him there on her doorstep makes her shudder. Must she let him in? She doesn't want to. But the look in his eyes tells her that he's going to enter. That he'll come in no matter what she does. He'll force his way in if he has to. She is well aware that she has no choice, but she resists all the same. She's always been hard-headed. What pretext can she find? "The... the children are sleeping..." Jean smiles. "I know... I know that, dear Madame, excuse me! I'm very late... Something came up. Unfortunately. I'm so sorry! You see, I have to talk to Daniel, right away, it can't wait, it's in his interest, you understand?" The old woman understands all too well, and in particular, she knows the true reason for Jean's visit. But how to stop him from coming in? She does not move from the door. She feels more and more ill at ease. What to do? Jean, all the time she's thinking, remains silent, upright, still smiling – certain that he'll be gaining access. But the old woman isn't done... doing the best she can... trembling. "It's just that Daniel isn't well... he's lying down... he's very tired. His work, you know? He's lying down... He has to sleep... He's sleeping. It would be better if you could... tomorrow ..." Jean shakes his head. No, he wants to see him now. Tomorrow will be too late. He shrugs again, falsely contrite, excuses himself, protests, and he has very important reasons, "really, believe me, I insist." And the old woman knows that she's lost. If it were a drunk or someone violent, she would know how to resist, throw him out, shut the door. But against this tall, unctuous individual, she doesn't know what to say. She backs off slowly. He steps inside, slowly as well "I... I'll go and get him." "Thank you."

Daniel was masturbating when he heard Jean come in. So, his penis deflated. His fantasies, his burning desires. Everything disappeared, leaving only the resonance of a metallic voice, and that of his mother, weak and suppliant, ready to capitulate. He got up. He dressed. Now he hears his mother's steps on the stairs. The cracking wood. And another crack, this one emanating from much further away, deep in his heart – he knows that this meeting will be decisive for Odette and for him, decisive "for us." "Daniel, Jean Pottier is downstairs, he wants to talk to you, says it's urgent." Yes. Yes. Daniel goes down. When he sees Jean sitting in his armchair, where no one has invited him to sit, Daniel first wants to retch, then, all the same, he moves towards Jean. "Ah... it's you." The old woman has come down as well. Jean smiles.

"My dear Daniel, I came as quickly as I could."

"You're bleeding."

Jean runs his hand over his temple, where the blood has dried, but is clearly visible. The old lady turns and examines him as well. She hadn't seen the blood. Now, in the light, she sees it clearly. It's on his temple, his chin, and even his clothes, yes, my God, he's covered in blood!

"What have you done?" she cries. "What have you done?"

The old woman leaps up. She runs to the cupboard where her husband kept, where there still is, his gun, his hunting rifle. "Mama!" cries Daniel, "Mama!" He rushes towards her, blocks her way, forces her to sit down. She struggles, she doesn't want to be pushed around, "No, no, let me go, no, Daniel." But Daniel is stronger. "Calm down, Mama."

Jean watches the scene without a word, amused by the sight of the night coming on, frayed and tattered. He senses what is to come. The far-off ramifications, enormous – the deep roots. He knows that everything is now beginning.

"It's nothing," he says calmly, "nothing at all. I hurt myself moving things around, furniture, what's left of my poor old man..."

It's true! His father hanged! And Daniel, in his distress, had said nothing to his mother. She doesn't know. She looks first at Jean, suspicious, and then at Daniel. What are they hiding from her? The gossip in her is appalled. What is it that she doesn't know?

"I just forgot... His father... His father is..."

"My father killed himself this morning," Jean cuts in.

The old woman is stupefied.

"Yes, the poor man, he hanged himself."

"Hanged?"

All of a sudden, she sees it, old Pottier, suspended from the ceiling, all black and grimacing – in this room, her living room! Under the fluorescents! – old Pottier hanged and presiding there, looking them up and down. Perhaps he's even grimacing, his lips moving, uttering insults and threats. The old woman harbours the super- stitions of the aged. And the omen chills her. She feels everything spinning round her. Swelling around her. Her feet slip away. The armchair lurches. "My God! My God!"

"Believe me. I would never have disturbed you if I didn't have good reason..."

And he remains impassive! And he dares to smile! But can he really? The snake wears a mask. She knows it. And Daniel sees nothing. He waits, half-afraid, half- confused. A silence sets in. One of those awkward moments that Jean enjoys so much. Daniel doesn't know quite what to say, in fact he has nothing at all to say since it's Jean who has come to talk to him. Finally, it's the old woman who, taking hold of herself, breaks the silence. Her son infuriates her. Why does he say nothing? Why does he never say anything? Why doesn't he know how to see and why does he always arrive too late? Since you don't want to talk, I'll talk. It's the moment to talk, Daniel. You're silent. But I won't be silent.

"Why have you come?"

"I told you. I had something important to tell Daniel. Except Daniel and I have to talk together, him and me, do you understand?"

55

The old woman understands. She's already known for some time that she has lost. Yet she still wants to persevere. To throw herself between Jean and her son. To assume the role of advocate, to defend him against the storm. She rises as best she can, heads painfully for the kitchen. Daniel looks at Jean, waits, he wants all this to end, wants Jean to be far away, for himself to be back in his bedroom with his thoughts of Odette.

"Not here," says Jean. "Let's go outside."

He exits. Daniel follows him. They're on the door-step.

"You know why I'm here?"

Daniel says he doesn't know.

"The blood, my friend. I didn't hurt myself all on my own. It's Odette ... Odette did this to me..."

Daniel cries out that it's not possible, it's not true, you're lying. Because Odette is so gentle. And so cheerful too. He can't imagine her convulsing in anger, being sad, being furious. Because in his dreams he allows Odette only one aspect. Often, when we think of the woman we love, day after day, we see just one expression, and the same sentence that she repeats, while we too pronounce only one.

"I assure you that it was her! She wanted to kill me. She went mad – drugged, and mad. I can't allow myself... my life is in danger. Who knows what she might still do?"

Daniel is afraid. Not for himself. But for her. It's been a long time since he's thought of himself. Other than through her.

"Where is she... Where is she? What have you done to her?"

"Her? She's fine! She's at home! She's perfectly fine! I'm the one who's hurt, understand? I'm the one she wanted to kill."

But Jean is the enemy.

"If she wanted to it's because..."

"What? That she was right to do it? I tell you she's crazy. This can't go on. She's dangerous, Daniel."

Daniel doesn't believe it. He knows Jean is lying. That he has it in for Odette and that he's lying to him. He'd like to tell him not to worry, even to dissemble a bit, say that he can hate Odette as much as he likes because he and Odette will soon be gone.

"Here's what you're going to do," says Jean. "You're going to denounce her, tomorrow. For her own good."

No! He will not denounce her.

"We have to stop her from hurting herself, and me – and you too. She's dangerous, Daniel. You may be impli-cated, of course, but I'll take care of everything. I'll testify. You won't go to prison. You'll be cleared! Not for one minute. I promise. I swear. I'll pay you enough from the old man's estate for you to win your trial."

No! He'll take her away.

Jean feels the flesh's resistance. Feels that his blade has hit a snag.

"I'm going to take her away."

Jean doesn't understand: take her away where? Why not accept the money? The others did. He has debts. Why not sell off Odette?

"Take her away? Take her away where?"

Daniel is brought up short. He doesn't know what to reply.

All right, Jean thinks to himself, he loves her, then what? What does that change? He's not that stupid!

Take her away! And then what! He tells him. That he's an idiot and that Odette, obviously, wouldn't go with him.

"Shut up! Shut up!"

But Jean has not come there to be silent. He pronounces the crucial sentence, no longer laughing.

"You're going to denounce her."

"I will not denounce her."

Jean is at his wit's end, dammit, what does this cretin want? He's digging in his heels!

"Then I will. You'll both go down."

"You won't do that."

"Oh yes I will."

And he looks Daniel in the face as Daniel, frightened, feels the ground slipping away under his feet. Jean smiles.

"And I'm the one that's fucking her. You hear me? Fucking her!"

Jean retreats. Too late. Daniel has him by the throat. Throws him backwards, crushes him under his weight, in the snow. Jean tries to speak. "Daniel! Daniel!" But Daniel can no longer hear. "You won't do that! You won't do that! You hear? You won't do that!" Jean tries again to cry out. He cannot. He's swallowing snow. "Daniel... Da..." Daniel repeats, "You won't do that." The door opens. His mother.

"Daniel! Stop! Daniel! Let him go!" A dog barks. The door of a neighbouring house opens as well. "Daniel! I beg you! Let him go!" A man in the shadows. Approaching. The barking. And Daniel blind and deaf, red in the face, incandescent in the cold night. "Daniel! Daniel!" His mother throws herself forward to separate them, the ice, she slips – she falls. Daniel doesn't hear her. Daniel hears no one. He just wants Jean to be quiet. To stop talking. Wants to stop him from harming her. Jean is saying nothing now, he's being strangled in Daniel's embrace. He tries to push Daniel off. Is he going to kill him? He thinks so. He's afraid. He'd like to beg him. To say no, he won't denounce him, he swears. He promises! He cannot... Daniel wants to kill him. He won't let him talk...His legs still move under Daniel's weight. His heels strike the ice. The old woman tries to rise. She screams, "Help! Help! Save my son!" It's the neighbour who takes Daniel by the waist, throws him to the side, separates them.

Jean gets up. He tries to stand straight. It's not easy. Daniel has stunned him. Badly. Meanly. Daniel spits on the ground. He says to his mother: "I didn't want that to happen. I'm sorry. But this can't go on." The old woman has known for a long time that this can't go on. Jean doesn't want to laugh now. Any more, he thinks, and these lunatics will keep me from going to Mexico. Odette, Daniel. To hell with them. He calculates, instinctively: from Tijuana, he'll send a letter to the Saint-Donat police. He'll accuse Odette and Daniel. Major traffickers. So, what if word gets around, if they find out that he too was involved. He'll be far away. The old woman is terrified. She's moaning. Please... Please... Jean says nothing. He gives the old woman a nod. Gets into his car. Daniel is sitting in the snow. He's no longer moving. He says nothing. Is he still thinking? First the storm, the wind, its howling. Then, nothing. Just the night. Black and silent. And that has entered his head.

*

Odette and Daniel are slipping towards the abyss that has opened up between what they are and what they would like to be. This cavernous void that each endures alone, where you can cry out but where your cry is never answered. The snow has stopped falling. The wind is no longer blowing. There are only men and the night. And the men cry out and the night is silent. On the rim of the cliff it would be hopeless to declare a winner, to say that this one will lose himself more than the other, or that that one will die, or another live. From high on the cliff, only losers can be seen. Losers who cry out. And the night that destroys them.

CHAPTER 5

The day before, when she heard the cry, she knew that there was nothing to be done. At her age, what more could she do? She knows what Jean's arrival means. The end of everything. All he's brought with him that is beyond redemption. And his father, hanged? Is he smiling under the fluorescents? No. Nothing more can be done. She helps Daniel get to his feet. Makes him some tea, as she did a while ago. The children have wakened so she puts them back to sleep. And she returns to her son, one hand on his shoulder, and waits for him to speak – but he says nothing. He clenches his fist. His gaze is dry. Hard. Hateful. As she has never known him. Something has changed. It's not rage anymore, but a covert desire to fight someone. A conscious and resolute desire to kill. He says nothing. Nor does she. She knows that he is gone, elsewhere. She knows what boundary he is about to cross. The fracturing. The final limit, the last pass. And he too knows it. His mother sighs. She'd like to cry. Life no longer allows her that. She wants to say something. This she can manage... She's used to lying... "Daniel... Daniel, don't, I beg you... It will all work out. Things can still be put in order." Maybe he would believe it if he could hear her, but he no longer does. He rises slowly. Without drinking his tea. Without seeing his mother. He climbs the stairs and shuts himself up in his room.

*

His room has changed. It's no longer the little cubbyhole that's peaceful and poor. The walls are oozing blood through their cracks. They swell and retract and pulse like a heart. The light of the fluorescents. And the odour is violent. Violence saturates the air in the room. It's unbearable. He goes towards the bed. In the middle of the room he turns around. The door is closed. Still other doors beyond this one are shut. The world drifts away. "So much the better," thinks Daniel. He is leaving the shore. Embarking with Odette and Jean, he sails far away into the night, drifting. The sky around him expands. Electrifies. Thunders. Daniel knows that all will be played out at the heart of the storm.

*

Odette, after Jean had pushed her into the snow, went home in tears, broke a glass table with a hammer blow, attacked the wallpaper with her nails, howled, swore, wept – and then she sat on her couch, quivering with rage. All those years of humiliation, prison, dirty looks, those of the judge – it all came back to her, flooded into her heart. All those years... Her position. Her embarrassment. And the huge black shadow of Jean. Who had just beaten her, once again, just when she wanted to show him. Show him what? Who she was? No, less than that – that she existed. But he hadn't seen. He'd got himself up. He'd laughed. She stayed there, on her back, for how long? She couldn't say. Several minutes, several hours? And he, where was he? He was celebrating. Or maybe not ... maybe he'd simply forgotten her. He must have forgotten. Had he ever known she was alive? If not, why had he not killed her?

*

Daniel calls Odette. He's beside himself. His voice. It shakes. Rants and raves. "Odette! Odette! It's you, Odette! He knows! Odette! He's going to talk! Us! I swear! Right there. In the snow. He'll tell everything! I strangled him, I killed him, no, I couldn't do it. Odette! I beg you. We have to leave. I don't know. I'll kill him. Oh! I swear, it was the neighbour. But if it weren't for my mother, he'd be dead, I swear! I swear to you! Odette!" At first, she doesn't comprehend, then through the cries, she thinks she understands. She tells him to be calm. "Calm down. Take your time. Daniel? Breathe."

"Jean came, right? And he threatened you."

"Yes. He said he'd denounce you. And I strangled him."

"He's not dead?"

"No."

Odette goes silent. The danger is there. Maybe Jean has already denounced her.

"Then I'll go to prison."

Daniel cries. No! She won't go to prison.

"But since he's gone... he'll denounce me tomorrow! Maybe tonight? I'll have the cops at my door!"

She imagines again the shame, the looks, the judge coming back at her, mocking her. She clenches her fists. She thinks she should have killed Jean. Even more, she thinks that it's Daniel who should have killed him. But he bungled it. He's the same cretin he always was. If only... Then she reflects. Maybe all is not lost. Her honour and her love. She says to Daniel:

"He must be at home..."

She doesn't understand his answer. He keeps fidgeting, words bubbling out of his mouth, incoherent but with one obsession: unless he stops Jean, Odette will go to prison. The idea drifts off, he loses track, he moans, his mind wanders, total delirium; then it returns, stronger still, shakes him to the core. "Odette, Odette, he's going to denounce you, we have to stop Jean, we have to silence him, Odette." Finally the idea comes clear, hardens, crystallizes around a single point: "I'll kill Jean."

And Odette says, "I love you."

*

He will kill Jean. Odette has hung up the phone. She's made things easy for him. She's convinced him. It's what he must do. He must see it through to the end. He will. He's promised her. Daniel has no choice, since his love hinges on this murder, his happiness, his whole small life.

Odette is pleased, she's jubilant. In the heat of the crime, she is happy. It's going to be over! She'll show him. Without soiling her hands. No more insults! Her revenge, her own!

She throws herself back on the couch. Her dress hiked up. She thinks of Jean, how he will be before he dies. At times very dignified. At times begging, moaning, that he be spared. She smiles. The thorn is being drawn from her heart, slowly, she feels it inching its way out, the sharp pain, the nerve. He, Jean, on the ground, so, are you still so proud? Which makes Odette laugh, the suffering that excites her, her nerves, the electric charge shooting through her. Are you still strutting? Where are your fists now? Are you looking at me? Eh? Why are you looking at me? Why did you never look at me? You knew who I was? Now you know, eh, now you know! She runs her hand over her vagina. Jean. Jean? Jean dead. Streaming from his heart along the blade. Droplets of blood. Of semen. She strokes herself, she moans, and Jean also moans, before he dies. He's off the road, Daniel beats him, makes him bleed, the snow is red. The ceiling above her is clouded, trembles, her vision blurs. She shivers. She's rolling around in death. So, Jean? So? Look! See me! See me! My eyes! She writhes from pleasure. The pleasure endures. At last. It sets in. The minutes. Spangles on her plaster ceiling. Mock stars. Ersatz death. Ready to crumble. And Jean collapses, defeated, killed for good. And she grows, she expands, she takes on unseemly dimensions, contours never imagined, sighing – Jean is dead. Jean is dead! She climaxes! She exists. She tears at the ceiling, at the stars. She is all of her life being born beneath her fingers, her vagina, at the side of the road where Jean is lying. The stirring of the galaxies. The heart within her explodes. Odette is alive at last.

*

"I'll kill him. I'll kill him. I'll kill Jean." Daniel is lying on his bed. The idea is clear, precise – acute. He can express it in its entirety. He can project it, live, along with the blood, Jean dead at the side of the road. "I'll kill him. I'll kill him." He imagines himself striking him. Twisting him. Breaking him. He imagines shooting him, face on, in the back, in his sleep, as he wakes. He imagines himself burning him alive. Knifing him, splitting his head in two. But all his various thoughts come together at one crossing point, his idea: "I will kill Jean." He is calm. The idea calms him. It's the first building block of his thought's edifice, his little edifice. From there he shapes that other thought, more clearly than he ever has: "I love Odette, I will kill Jean." He likes the formulation that has come to him. He relishes the words. At last! The words that were blocked, held in for so long. That free themselves in his thought stream, in the flow of solid words. "I will kill Jean." He makes ready. He raises his head. He feels as though he's in the act of accomplishing something.

Daniel gets up. Dresses. Goes down the stairs. His mother hears him. She knows where he's going. She trembles, but what can she do, a poor old woman? Since he doesn't listen to her, she'll say nothing. Daniel leaves the house. He gets into his pick-up truck, with the scoop raised. He starts the engine. He leaves. The old woman stays in the shadows, motionless, beaten down.

*

Jean looks at himself in the mirror, he's bleeding under his chin, it gives him a red collar, he smiles at himself, charms himself.

When will he denounce them? Tomorrow? Why not right away? Or Friday, after the old man is buried? He passes his hand under his chin, his palm is red, he looks at it. Or maybe he won't denounce them, it's true, nothing's forcing him. The fact is that he *can* denounce them.

He daydreams. His mirror. Maybe Odette will put a rope around her neck. More likely she'll scream at the police who have come for her and then go silent. And Daniel? That fat cretin? Will he expire in his mother's skirts? Or will he end up killing her, in anger? His ridiculous love for Odette! "He wants to take her away! On a horse no doubt, she side-saddle, what a laugh! I wonder where they'd go!" It's true, where would they go, supposing she agreed to leave? He sees them first in the city, Montreal, then Trois-Rivières, finally in Mexico, where his own fantasies lie. But no. His imagination is running away with him. His good will. He can't see them together. Odette, Daniel. It's impossible. There are people who ought to stay apart. He concludes that it's all nonsense and he laughs some more. But all the same! Goddamn Daniel! The fat idiotic brute! How could he be so stupid? It's that the heart puts down roots so deep that Jean cannot detect them. He has no idea. The fine traceries of love escape him. He doesn't know how to love. He knows nothing of what one can find deep in the heart. He doesn't see how sometimes it can be very strange. Myself, I've seen a couple in tears embracing on a railway station platform, he handsome and tall and rather well dressed, she ugly and old. I burst out laughing. Just like that, I told myself that they had no idea. But if they were weeping, it's because they were right.

Jean doesn't love. He screws his girlfriend now and then, a man has needs, it's hygiene. Just for appearance's sake, Sabrina sometimes reproaches him for being cold and insensitive. He answers with a kick. And she goes silent. She sighs a little. But she doesn't love him either. What she likes is the sex and that he pays for her in restaurants. They don't ask for anything more. Their Mexican future is a materialistic dream. It's above all the hacienda near the sea, the home entertainment system, and the big meals they'll make. There's no feeling beyond what it takes to flip your lid, scream as loud as you can, hammer the wall. They lack grace, lightness. They know nothing of tragedy. Inner torment. Its ramifications. Odette's rage. Daniel's. Their roads are paved. They ride towards the sun! Jean will sing in the car, a convertible, with his guitar, and Sabrina will giggle and sing as well. They'll hear themselves in the music.

He washes his face, disinfects it. He sits in front of the TV, opens a beer. He drinks while he watches a hockey game. He forgets about his projects, becomes absorbed in his own comfort, his head spins a little, Odette is far away, Daniel too. A second beer and over-time. Then Jean sleeps – his father's watch on his wrist.

*

Daniel hasn't killed anyone. A sheet of ice. A gust of wind. Distraction. He left the road. The car in the snow, the wheels spinning, he's stuck.

I'm on my way back from Montreal when I find him. I see a car sticking out of the ditch. I stop. Cries. Daniel has got out and he's pounding the metal, yelling, crying too. All his anger flying off into the night. The fir trees tremble. He knows that he has lost Odette, that Jean has escaped – that there's nothing to be done. He's grasped it all instinctively. He knows that he won't kill tomorrow. It all had to have happened tonight. He's lost his chance. I call to him, timidly: "Daniel, Daniel." But he doesn't answer. He kicks at the snow, he digs in, he falls, he gets up – and always, his cries of rage. I call again: "Daniel, hey, Daniel! Can you hear me?"

A car passes without stopping. "Daniel!" His cries become moans, sobs. Daniel is on his knees in the snow, his head against the fender of his pick-up truck. I go closer. Lay my hand on his shoulder. He turns around. Stares at me. His eyes are full of tears. His face is hard to look at. "She's gone," he says, sobbing. He knows he's been wrenched from her, and that they'll never run away together. That she will follow her road, and he'll follow his. That they've come to a parting of the ways. Two knees in the snow against his Chevrolet. He doesn't talk of Jean. He only talks of her. What she will say. I'd like to take him in my arms, but I don't know, my heart isn't in it. "Come on Daniel, I'll take you back, we'll come for your car tomorrow, it'll be daytime." He doesn't want to leave. He wants his failure to sink in. He wants to assume it entirely. Drink it to the dregs. Get drunk on himself. His obliteration. The ditch. His whole being plummeting down. He feels so little. Odette will tell him as much tomorrow, soon. He knows it already. That he has lost his chance to live. The night will close in on him. All his blood. And the storm will be over.

*

We're finally on the road, him and me. He doesn't say a word. He sobs onto the seat. He shakes a lot. Like a child. But a child who's gone too far.

When we arrive, his mother rushes towards us, tears in her eyes. She's understood right away that her son has killed no one, that Jean is alive. She'd had no more hope. She was resigned. Life has its surprises! She smiles. She even jokes. Her Daniel still wails a little, he's a child in crisis, but it will pass, as they have all passed. Tomorrow she'll hold him against her. And she'll speak the words he needs: "Daniel, drink, Daniel, eat, forget it all, Daniel, forget." And she thinks that he'll drink, that he'll eat, and that he'll think about it no more. The old woman is taking joy in her miracle. She pushes Christ to the limit. Reels off her hypotheses. The strands of this mystery. But I don't smile. Daniel says not a word. He goes up to his room. He will speak no more.

The old woman makes coffee. She pats me on the back. Tells me how happy she is that I brought Daniel home. Now everything will be better. I say yes, it will all be better. But I'm not so sure. There will be more storms, of that I'm certain. Odette and Daniel, where will their whirlwind lead them? They will face what skies? All the ice is honed into thin black blades. That lie in wait for them. That are promised to them. There is a mustering of blood. And I fear for them. It's best to say nothing. To close oneself in. To lower one's pen. My prose in the wind. Nothing. No, nothing. Never take up arms against silence.